MW00933606

Shanti and the Knot of Protection

A Rakhi Story

written by
Amita Roy Shah

illustrated by
Faariha Mastur

2023 Copyright - Amita Roy Shah.
All Rights Reserved

No part of this book may be reproduced,
stored in a retrieval system, or transmitted
by any means without the written
permission of the author.

ISBN: 9798396596597

First Published - 2023
Amita Roy Shah

Illustrator: Faariha Mastur
www.faarihamastur.com

This book is dedicated to my niece Saraya and to my children, Lara and Deven.

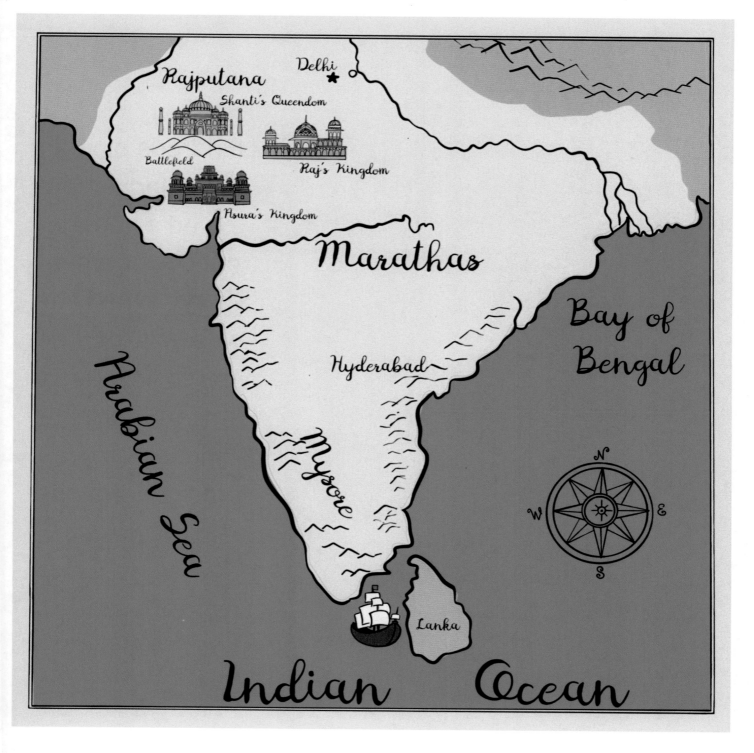

Hundreds of years ago in India there lived a young princess named Shanti. When she was only 14, her parents voyaged to Lanka. Sadly, they encountered a terrible storm and their ship sank.

When Shanti's parents died, she became one of the few queens to rule in India—and at only 14, this made her the youngest queen in India to have inherited a kingdom. As the new queen, Shanti made an announcement. "I will lead my new queendom according to the four greatest values my parents have taught me," she said. "Strength, curiosity, community, and security."

Shanti's queendom was secured by four pillars. One in the north, one in the east, one in the south, and one in the west.

She named each pillar after one of the four values, believing that these values would guide her in making important decisions for her queendom.

The north pillar was the pillar of strength. To make her body strong, Shanti often challenged herself to long runs. After her long runs, she would often look at herself in the mirror and say, "I am strong. I am brave. I am courageous."

Shanti knew it was especially important to be a strong leader because of the evil conqueror Asura, who was trying to take over territories that had precious gems.

Shanti's queendom had the rarest diamonds in the world—red diamonds, which were kept secure below the palace.

The east pillar was the pillar of curiosity, which Shanti had plenty of herself. If someone couldn't find Shanti, it was often because she was in the library trying to find an answer to her favorite question: "Why does it have to be this way?" This question always led her to new discoveries.

The south pillar was the pillar of community. After Shanti's parents died, her uncles and aunts came together to help raise her. As a ruler, she wondered to herself, "Why don't the other kings and queens come together like this, to help one another in case of an attack?"

With this in mind, Shanti set off one day on her horse, Toofan. She traveled to the closest kingdom, where she met with King Raj.

Shanti was determined to create an alliance and boldly asked, "If Asura invades my queendom, can I count on you to protect us against the evil Asura?"

In that moment, King Raj realized that if Asura invaded Shanti's queendom, his kingdom could be next—for his kingdom had valuable blue sapphires that were hidden away in a cave.

When King Raj agreed to Shanti's idea, she tore a piece of her sari and tied it to his wrist. As she tied it, she proclaimed, "This is a knot of protection. This knot is a reminder of your promise to keep my queendom safe from any threats."

King Raj agreed and replied, "Yes, this knot represents my promise to protect your queendom."

As Shanti had expected, Asura soon came
to invade. Shanti flashed a light from the
south pillar—the pillar of community—

signaling to King Raj that she needed his help. King Raj immediately prepared his army and protected Shanti's queendom.

It wasn't until the day that King Raj came to her aid that Shanti truly understood the importance of the west pillar—the pillar of security.

After King Raj came to her aid, Shanti decided to set aside one day every year to honor the knot of protection —the rakhi—that had signified the promise she and King Raj made to protect each other.

Today, Rakhi is a celebration that honors the special bond between siblings, cousins, and friends both near and far.

They celebrate their bond each year by tying a rakhi, exchanging presents, and eating sweets.

More About Rakhi (pronounced rah-kee)

Rakhi is a Hindu festival that celebrates brother-sister relationships and the love siblings have for each other. It is celebrated annually, when there is a full moon in the Hindu lunar calendar month of Shravan, which is usually in August. Rakhi is also known as Raksha Bandhan, a term from Sanskrit that translates as "bond of protection."

During Rakhi, a sister ties a rakhi to her brother's right wrist. The rakhi signifies a sister's bond with and support of her brother. In exchange, the sister receives her brother's promise of protection; this is often accompanied with a gift. After the gift has been exchanged, the sister feeds her brother his favorite Indian sweets, such as ladoos, jalebis, phirni, kaju katli, or gulab jamun.

Traditionally, the rakhi was tied only by sisters to brothers. But as times have changed, we are finding new ways to celebrate and keep Raksha Bandhan as a part of our rich cultural heritage. Nowadays, siblings of the same gender may tie rakhis to one another, younger siblings may tie rakhis to their older siblings, and an only child may tie rakhis to cousins or friends with whom they share a close bond. Many children also mail rakhis to those who don't live nearby.

By keeping in touch in this way, children are able to honor the special relationships they have with one another even though they may live far apart. Allowing Rakhi traditions to change with the times ensures that the children of future generations will continue to celebrate it, knowing that they are safe, that they will be protected, and that they have many allies—both near and far—to support them in times of need.

More About the Origins of Rakhi

This story, *Shanti and the Knot of Protection,* is a fictional story loosely based on legends and historical stories about the origins of Rakhi.

Rani Karnavati and Emperor Humayun

The legend of Rani (or Queen) Karnavati and Emperor Humayun is one closely tied to Rakhi. After Queen Karnavati's husband—King Rana Sanga—died, she ruled over Mewar. When Bahadur Shah of Gujarat attacked Mewar for the second time, Queen Karnavati began looking for support from other kingdoms. She wrote to Emperor Humayun for help, sending him a rakhi and asking for his protection. He did go to Mewar to help, but unfortunately did not make it in time.

Roxana and King Porus

Another common story related to Rakhi is that of Roxana and King Porus. This story—based on actual historical events—dates back to 300BC, when Alexander the Great was ready to conquer India. His wife, Roxana, was worried for his safety, for she knew he would have to battle Porus, the king of the Pauravas. Roxana sent a rakhi to King Porus, asking him not to hurt her husband on the battlefield. At one point during the Battle of the Hydaspes River, King Porus noticed the rakhi on his wrist and was reminded of his promise to Roxana. He then stopped himself from attacking Alexander. Though King Porus lost the battle, he won Alexander's respect. Afterwards, Alexander reinstated Porus as the governor of what had been his kingdom.

A list of Hindi words in this book–

- *asura*: demon

- *raj*: king

- *rakhi*: knot or bracelet

- *raksha bandhan*: bond of protection

- *rani*: queen

- *sari*: a strip of cloth, a garment made up of lightweight cloth draped so that one end forms a skirt and the other a shoulder covering, worn by many South Asian women

- *shanti*: peace

- *toofan*: storm

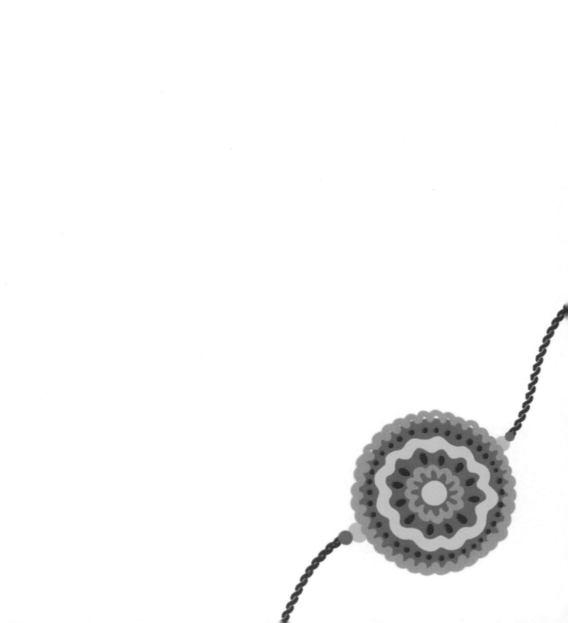

How to Make a Braided Rakhi

① Select three pieces of thread or embroidery floss. The red color is symbolic of the fire element and is traditionally used to signify security and protection in the relationship.

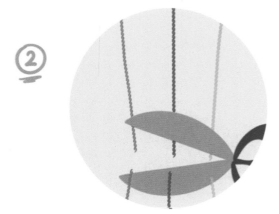

② Cut enough of each string so that it will fit around your rakhi sibling's right wrist, about 10 inches.

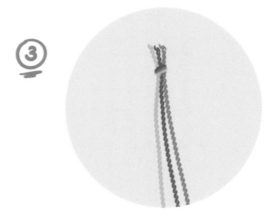

③ Hold your threads together at one end and make a small knot.

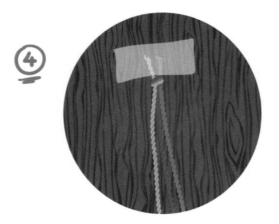

④ Tape the knotted end to a table.

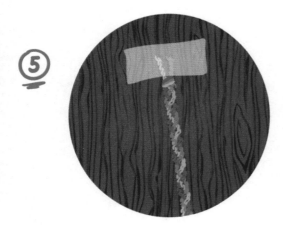

⑤ Starting at the knot, braid the rest of the strings.

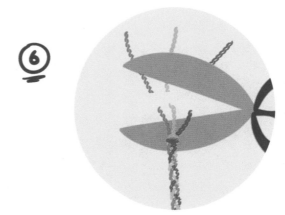

⑥ When you are finished braiding, tie another knot and trim the ends.

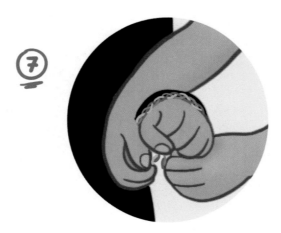

⑦ You are ready to tie the rakhi (your knot of protection) on your sibling, friend, or cousin!

How to Make a Personalized Rakhi

①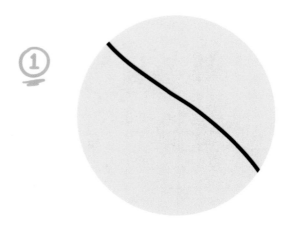

Get one piece of string or yarn.

②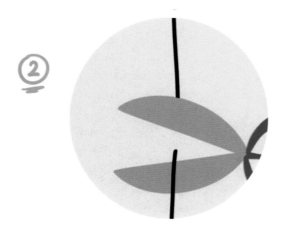

Cut enough string so you can make sure the personalized letters are in the middle of the string, about 10 inches.

③

Buy personalized letter beads from the store. It can be the letters to spell the name of the person you are giving your rakhi to, or more traditionally it could be BHAI, which stands for brother in Sanskrit.

④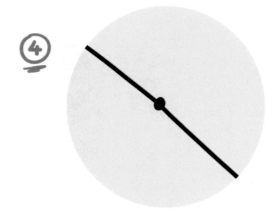

Tie a knot just over halfway on the thread.

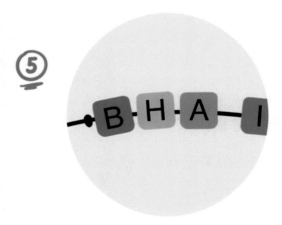

Add your beads of choice.

Tie another knot at the other end of
the beads and trim the edges to
desired finished length.

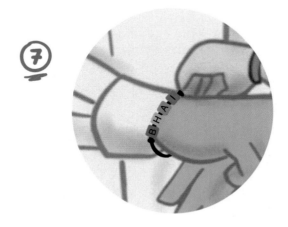

You are now ready to tie the rakhi
(your knot of protection) on your sibling,
friend, or cousin!

Made in the USA
Coppell, TX
20 September 2023

21787190R00024